KING PIG

For Niah, Elan, Tais and Ezra

Scholastic Canada Ltd.
604 King Street West, Toronto, Ontario M5V 1E1, Canada

Scholastic Inc.
557 Broadway, New York, NY 10012, USA

Scholastic Australia Pty Limited
PO Box 579, Gosford, NSW 2250, Australia

Scholastic New Zealand Limited
Private Bag 94407, Botany, Manukau 2163, New Zealand

Scholastic Children's Books
Euston House, 24 Eversholt Street, London NW1 1DB, UK

www.scholastic.ca

Library and Archives Canada Cataloguing in Publication
Bland, Nick, 1973-
King pig / written and illustrated by Nick Bland.
ISBN 978-1-4431-2486-7 (bound).–ISBN 978-1-4431-2487-4 (pbk.)
I. Title.
PZ7.B557Ki 2013   j823'.92   C2012-907801-8

Published in Australia by Scholastic Press, 2013
This edition published in Canada by Scholastic Canada Ltd., 2013

Text and illustrations copyright © 2013 by Nick Bland

6 5 4 3 2 1   Printed in Malaysia 108   13 14 15 16 17

KING PIG

Nick Bland

Scholastic Canada Ltd.
Toronto New York London Auckland Sydney
Mexico City New Delhi Hong Kong Buenos Aires

King Pig could never understand why the sheep didn't adore him. They were always complaining about one thing or another.

They hardly ever smiled,

and when they did, King Pig
thought they were teasing him.

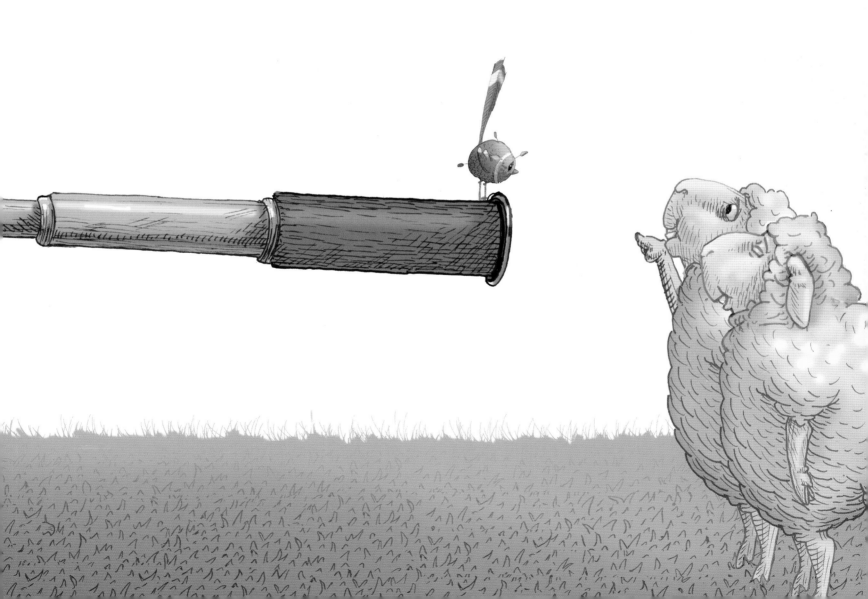

They never listened properly,
no matter how loudly he shouted.

And the harder
he tried to get
their attention . . .

the more they ignored him.

Because he was the king, he could make the sheep
do whatever he wanted . . .

whenever he pleased.

But he just couldn't
make them *like* him.

"Maybe they would like me more if I looked . . . fancier," said King Pig. For that, he would need a lot of fancy new clothes.

But who could he get to make them?

King Pig woke up all the sheep
and invited them into his nice,
warm castle.

And there he slept while the sheep went to work.
They gathered up every last snippet of their wool,

and they knit, knit, knitted all through the night
until the king had his pile of fancy new clothes.

In the morning, King Pig was ready to prance.
He looked . . .

He was ferocious.

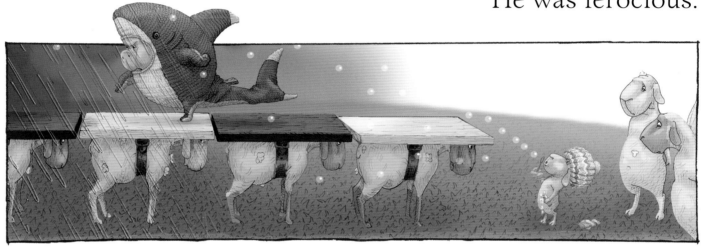

He was fearless.

He was the best-dressed king in the kingdom.

But when he stopped to take a bow, nobody was watching.

Nobody was cheering. Nobody was *adoring* him.

"Maybe you could try being nice," said a little voice.

"But I thought I *was* being nice!" said King Pig,
and he went inside to sulk.

That night, King Pig couldn't sleep.
He felt something he'd never felt before.

He felt sorry.

Then, at last, he thought of something
nice he could do for the sheep.

He worked
through the night

and into the morning.

By sunrise, he was
ready to say sorry
in the only way
he could think of.

It wasn't perfect, but all the sheep agreed . . .

it was a pretty good start.